California Brown

California Brown

Illuminations and Hollers, 2008-2024

Juan Felipe Herrera

MOUTHFEEL PRESS

"Meet the poem head on, Glomski!"
                    Jerry Stern in the Writers Workshop, University of Iowa

For Itzolín, great young poet from New Mexico, gone too soon, RIP.

For Gerald Stern & Marvin Bell, RIP, my poetry profs & friends, Writers Workshop, University of Iowa, 1988-1990.

"¿Vicente, a dónde va la gente?"

— Tío Roberto Quintana, radio host, KOFY
"El Vocero del Pueblo" — SF. 1950s-60s.

"Tienes una estrella en la frente." "You have a star on your forehead."
— Mamá Lucha, Lincoln Road, Escondido, CA, 1955

For my mother, Lucha Herrera Quintana (1904-1986)
For my father, Felipe Emelio Herrera (1882-1964)

Dedications

For Margarita de Las Flores, even before day one—
Para mis hijas e hijos, nietos y bisnietos — for all my familias — amor y más amor
For our poets, artists, composers & friends that have passed away — Janice
Mirikitani, Al Young, José Montoya, Bobby Paramo, Rodrigo Reyes, Victor Martinez,
Francisco X. Alarcón, Ramón "Chunky" Moroyoqui Sánchez, Alfonsito Texidor, QR
Hand, Jack Hirschman, Bruno Louchouarn, Tony Ryan & Juan Pablo Gutierrez,
Rest in Love
For my sisters & familia passed on in the last few years — Sarita Chavez, Concha
Aguilar Contreras, David Herrera & my brother-in-law, Ricardo Chavez.
For my sobrino, Dicky Chavez & sobrina Chris Gomez-Valdez, Love forever.
For Fresno
For all the poets, ¡punto!
For Paul Flores, the Biala Pamilia, CPITS poets of La Mission, SF, Before Columbus
Foundation, University of Tucson, AZ, Poetry Center
For the Chavez family in Long Beach, Herrera Families in El Paso, Soma Mei Pirata,
Quantum DanceWord Ensemble, Linda Tomko
For Alvinita & Ed, Tito (RIP), Judy, Julie & Dave, Yolanda, Julian, Vicente (RIP), Rosita
(RIP), & Muñoz Familia
Love and Gratitude, Peace & Kindness for this world & the universe
For the Dalai Lama, for your Dharma teachings & the Sangha
For all migrants, DACA, immigrants, U are free, this is also your land!
For all my dear friends, thru the years—
For Maria Miranda Maloney, publisher of Mouthfeel Press
For Corey Madden & Team at Monterey Art Museum
For Kendra Marcus & Minju & for Anya, Rebecca & Miyako & Blue Flower Arts
For Tom Lutz & Laurie, Roberto Alvarez, Bilazo, Amalia & Kareninna & El Venado
For Alfredo Arreguín (RIP) & Suzy, gracias for your art & mural at JFH Elementary, Fresno
For Lauro Flores & Familia & Lalo Borja gracias for your translations & friendship
For Cody & Mai Der, JJ, Rosaldo & Mary, Medrano, Bianka, Ceci, Marisol, Lee,
Dominguez, Campos, Liz Acevedo, Bosch, Borjas and all the Labbers
For the Martinez Families
For my Library of Congress Homies
For Governor Newsom & First Partner of California — Jennifer Siebel Newsom
For the Poetry Foundation, ¡Gracias, gracias, gracias!
For the Academy of American Poets — many appreciations — We had a blast!
For the Poetry Society of America — abundant gratitude
For the Urrea Familia
For Chicano Park, Mando Nuñez & Familias
For Hmong Writer's Club, MFA's & CSUF Laureate Labbers, Fresno
For all my publishers & teachers, ¡Gracias!
For all that have invited me to speak with open arms — I bow to you
For Principal Dr. Miguel Naranjo & VP Sarah Chavez & teachers at JFH Elementary,
¡mil gracias!
For the Earth that holds us, accepts us, nourishes us — ¡Viva!
For all my teachers & mentors.

Brown Table

My Mother's Name is Lucha — 1
We Shall Build a New House Green — 2
Construiremos una nueva casa verde — 3
SunRiders — 6
JinetesSolares — 7
Aztec In-Visions — 8
60 Miles from Tepic, Nayarit, Mexico/
Ochre Yellow Green Stone Huichol Campo, 1970 — 10
Dolphinating — 12
Mahler – Son Borne of a Street Song — 13
Mural Poem on "Mural" by Jackson Pollock — 14
Migra con pistola, una riata y caballo
Border Guard Man with a Gun, a Riata & a Horse — 15
Poema de la frontera en cartón — 21
Active Shooter — 23
Las Atenco Eleven — 25
Nohemi — Song for Paris — 27
For George Floyd Was a Great Man — 30
Porque George Floyd era un gran hombre — 31
i Will Luv U 4Ever, Orlando — 32

Crossing Poland to Hope 34
Dawn Will Usher Me 38
La aurora me guiará 39
Libélula / Dragonfly 42
The Enlightenment of William Shatner in Space 48
La iluminación de William Shatner en el espacio 49
Mind Core 52
Walking Notes (Tenochtitlán, DF)
with Francisco X. Alarcón, 1978 54
Ramón "Chunky" Moroyoqui Sánchez Played 57
Tutu Sol — At the Underground Café 58
California Brown 61
Notice: Stop Anti-Semitism 63
Landing on Earth Tomorrow 64
HOLLER / GRITO 66
PRONOUN(CE) ME 72

Notes / Credits **77**

California Brown

My Mother's Name is Lucha

your hands my hands

kindnesses   dances   silences sitting   you i

        El Paso Texas   Segundo Barrio

Juárez   1918   1936 in gypsy   dress actress

you sing   i sing we sing   lullabies of old

this   now lines now   my birth

heart now life

                              all life   now

              i   bow   to you

We Shall Build a New House Green

An Anthem for Health Care Without Harm

We shall build a new house green we shall
build it with oceans & eucalyptus leaves with
the agreements of all things it shall be
                                a healing house

                        the healing shall be for all
breathing free children climate breathing free
fossil fuel gone & gas & oil & coal gone
in every floor there will be a bowl of kindness

nurses & emergency room doctors & first responders
at the center of every community this house green
at the center of every nation & island radiating beyond
can you see it now it will be a fountain it will be

                a source of compassion a floor w/o carbon
the walls & rooms & stations w/o plastic we shall
build it with the permission of the mountains of thunder face
the stirring light of immeasurable dreams of all realized

                our house shall flourish green & solarizing
flowers solarizing hope solarizing Earth its cities in crises
as the Arctic Wolf prowling for sustenance on the
last snow sliding on the watery shards of permafrost

our eyes shall cast their gaze upon the lives
of all w/wholeness w/o micro-poisons
piercing the cells & span of all living beings
all shall taste the joyous flower of life yes

Construiremos una nueva casa verde

Un Himno para Grupo Health Care Without Harm

Construiremos una nueva casa verde
hecha de mares y hojas de eucalipto con
el acuerdo de todos será

                    una casa de curación

                la curación será para todos
niños respirando libremente clima respirando liberado
combustible fósil desaparecido y gas y
petróleo y carbón desaparecido
en cada piso habrá un cántaro de cordialidad

enfermeras y médicos de urgencias y socorristas
en el centro de cada comunidad esta casa verde
en el centro de cada nación e isla radiando más allá
puedes verla ahora será una fuente será

           un manantial de compasión un piso sin carbón
las paredes y cuartos y estaciones sin plástico la
construiremos con permiso de las montañas de truenos
ante la luz vivaz de los innumerables sueños de tantos hechos realidad

          nuestra casa florecerá verde y solarizante
flores solarizadas esperanza solarizada la Tierra sus ciudades en crisis
como el lobo ártico en busca de alimento en las últimas nieves
deslizándose sobre astillas de permafrost

nuestros ojos fijarán su mirada en la vidas
de todos con harmonía sin micro-venenos
que perforan las células y existencias de todo ser viviente
todos probarán la jubilosa flor de la vida sí

we shall know happiness we shall know the healing
of earth & sky we shall know the liberation
of HCFC's we shall witness our existence genuine
we shall build this house with the New Idea

      how to bend time with our hearts and mind
each one of us tasking unity humanity &
the planetary scope of compassion, ethics
perseverance and radical re-imagination

      in every hall in every room in every
foundation & roof in every beam in every
interconnection & network & weaving
there will be nature & peoples breathing
there shall be a rainbow garden of ancestral offerings
we shall open the doors of our healing house green
there shall be a choir in movement in harmony
many lives will survive & sing hope in every space

      the healing for all
        the future saved
          the voice of all
            life granted & shared &
              the planet Earth holy

we shall build this house w/ incandescent sky
the wisdom of life shall be painted on every pathway
w/ Giant Sequoia leaves w/ ocean songs determined
& courageous for humanity healing healing

            turquoise & green

conoceremos la felicidad conoceremos la sanación
de la tierra y el cielo conoceremos la liberación
de los HCFCs presenciaremos nuestra genuina existencia
haremos esta casa con la Nueva Idea

        cómo curvear el tiempo con nuestro corazón y mente
cada uno de nosotros encomendando unidad humanidad y
compasión a medida planetaria, la ética
perseverancia y una re-imaginación radical

        en cada pasillo en cada cuarto en cada
cimiento y techo en cada viga en cada
cruce y red y tejido
habrá naturaleza y la respiración de todos
habrá un jardín de arcoiris de ofrendas ancestrales
abriremos las puertas de nuestra casa verde curación
habrá un coro en movimiento en armonía
muchas vidas sobrevivirán y cantarán la esperanza en todo lugar

        la curación para todos
          el futuro rescatado
            la voz de todos
               vida ofrendada y compartida y
                 el planeta Tierra sagrado

construiremos esta casa con cielo brillante
la sabiduría de la vida estará pintada en cada camino
con hojas de secoya gigante y canciones de mar resolutas
y valientes para la humanidad curándose curándose

        turquesa y verde

"Go, goooo

Lucy!"

everyone back home cheered

miles millions we circled

Trojans, Jupiter's eye, El Sol

2,000, 000 years

sun riders

made of hope —

love?

Earth was

divided

there was hate

there was sickness

Arctic sliding

we gathered we flourished

kindness healed us

Lucy carried us

tumbling through planetesimal trails

love saved us

who will we   be?

compassion

science

humanity —

Light

Jinetes Solares

"¡Vaaamos,

                    Lucy!"

     todo mundo gritaba desde casa

millas millones rodeamos

asteroides troyanos, el ojo de Júpiter, El Sol

    2,000,000 años   jinetes del sol

       hechos de esperanza—   amor?

    La tierra   dividida

había odio   habían enfermedades

el deshielo del ártico   ncs unimos y florecimos

           el corazón de todos nos curó

      Lucy nos condujo

tumbos robóticos por senderos planetesimales   el amor nos salvó

¿en quiénes nos convertiremos?

         compasión

                ciencia

         humanidad —

            Luz

Aztec In-Visions

In memory of Francisco X. Alarcón, Victor Martinez & JPG

After   the reading Centeotl   i

noticed we & during calpulli the reading of

poetas del pueblo copál

at La Plaza de Las Tres Culturas LA

our   voices had multiplied Coyolxauki

ocelotl comal sartén tacuche   our rockface our

voices
            had been condor-wing-brushed colored

                    Popocatépetl in warrior

penacho sky bolt — though

aúnque   as José Montoya

                    used to say aúnque

that *is*

                    jade sacrifice canto — our voice Ollin Jazz

had attained corregimiento alcalde Nezahualcóyotl

                    encomienda something cut new Ranchera

after so many yrs
                                    walking

round danza

temazcal confessions

metate   Ilhuicamina peregrinaje

                                        Malinche

                                        Malinche

                                        malinalli
our river río

        El Santiago Huichol Cora & Tepehuana

El Lerma Honduras El Grande El Paso

                        we were breathing fire trains

                        we were sewing maíz azul

                bathing in its blaze bluish life

                we were

        gathering blessing brilliance Tlalok

        our faces in gentle casa colors Toltecatl esmeralda skull

                                in the complexity open

raining our dresses and nakedness ombligo Leunar

Huehueteotl Xóchitl you   we   again

60 Miles from Tepic, Nayarit, Mexico /
Ochre Yellow Green Stone Huichol Campo, 1970

Tied to you & then not tied then unwound & then painted then
Told not told & not told then risen & painted

Let's See:

> Ochre yellow green stone Huichol campo
> pink yarn pressed wax from Campeche
> Tipeyote Tipeyote Giver of Visions we walk
> Peyoteros Peyoteros
we know how to walk so we walk we walk

At the
The edge
At the edge
At the edge of the city where there is no city for us you now
> Where retreat is city & hole adobe is city & fence & dirt is

See this string
Take this string
Pull this string
Turn this string

Walk away pull & pull & pull & twine & take estambre you with   Me
Sit
Now you (this is how you find you walk how you find you find walk life
Who knows this? You will know)

Sit now you
Sit
I sit you sit
I sit you sit & turn this string this color sky fire Grandfather Fire string
Grandfather Tatewarí first story of Huichol Wíxarika string fire string
So
So   so it can flame story so it can flame you back First People
                                    so you can tell story on the wall in the sky

Ahh ahh ahh
Ohh ohh ehh sheee   shee up mountain

                                            —*Warrior Woman Valley, Nevada*

Dolphinating

For Albert Goldbarth & Margarita Luna Robles

Are you going to steal lines collect
manual typewriters 8 miles high the serotonin Albert
Goldbarth mentions the sugary night the howling
speeding most of all are you going to hobble here—
                              time travel?
a possible future burns your dolphin karma
forking out 500 lives from now
Whitman in pajamas spotted leopard-like piercing
the unavoidable Void the obsessed B-B-Q where we swoop

Ersatz

    Mojo

       Bruja   Hoodoo scribble

it is popping Hendrix in your head it is Joplin &
Flor Silvestre & Rosetta Tharpe & Itzpapalotl do you know
how awake you are

                  Noble
               8 Fold Path

too dark
too lightning
the visualization is next
the Ukrainian purge the intercontinental money money
O Tsunami where is my crystal-realized selfie
      O my love my next Warhol dream in
   revolution rouge & where is
my electric emerald wand rain Vajra
roll the ink & fire stones   unfold the third eyes
the ten million arms of Tara & Einstein
of compassion of mercy of nebula rails come alive
jellyfish flags i bow to you
        jellyfish world wheel of
swish & suffering

Mahler – Son Borne of the Street Song

Inspired by the life of Gustav Mahler & his last Symphony #9

in the darkness,

in the exile — there is a sigh, a number 9

there is a son borne of street song, the injured tympani red drum

there is a town *Jihlava*, a make-shift theatre &

rough-cut street dancers, there is a sky that welcomes him

his furious strings tasking the universe, his weaving of all things

the piccolo & the flute

oboes of furies tiny streams of burning slow breath

we wait in silence & face up

we notice the heavens the turbulence &

wild sharp strokes & pieces of banned color & banned voices

their outcast Jewish hymn takes us to the endless seas

unknown choruses unknown winds & collapsing worlds

we enter we follow we enter we halt we are halted

vanishing harmonies you walk through quadrants of space

music what is it one note encompasses everything

one oboe returns why

your life beginning your life almost ending then ending

what do you hear in this vastness this movement before you

unknown forces whirl violins & the dead

the director's arms & hands sway shaking point dissolve

only still we stand now we only

left alone only Gustav Mahler lives on

by this bed this night this day this last cycle

falls into an ever-returning descent of sound

a voice a voice do you hear it hear it

Mural Poem on "Mural" by Jackson Pollock

The mural the machine the odd angled multi-headed splash brush & can
mobile Siqueiros Mexican muralista tears through the canvas wall & his
fingertips smash your eyes it is south to north it is borderlessness it is
two nations Become One workshops in MEXICA town you are there &
there is here & you notice the walls the buildings the ancient Aztec stone
stelae the urgent lands now called Mexico City there is exchange painter to
painter colors to colors brush to brushes fury to fury that endless energy
star system of blood pour out onto earth & its peoples galleries & grasses
walls walks & pyramids the canvas down below we continue we search for
a name a face a body a warrior a ceremonial marriage with hearts hearts
hearts above & across the moment calls us the tectonics shift us the ocean
explodes the people are searching dreaming surrounding each other we
touch the stones you touch the fires you enter the abyss the mouth the
lava of the earth pour pour pour out onto the floors that are not floors
bend kneel pour the figures rise twist merge blur above below we drive
you something unknown comes to you we smear our faces into each other
the vastness ignites the mitosis shoots we lean forward & backward at the
same time can you hear the birthing can you see the trail there is no trail
this is the experiment this is the unknown speaking natives & steel head
dresses & serpents Coatlicue Goddess of the Earth Kahlo with Tehuantepec
weaving stitched on her chest Diego Rivera ascends the wall of City College
of San Francisco Paula Goddard wife of Charlie Chaplin we are all here your
flaming hands your flaming body your flaming orchestras go down The
Mural the prophecy the big picture contains us all the living the dead the
grand experiment it is here we shall go now today this very minute we go
in all directions there is a tsunami here it is a Changing there is the embryo
of Frank O'Hara & his easy cutting mind across the avenues round & round
he goes we go up up up up we raise our heads all in one stream & another
you don't stop you continue the paint has been emptied yet it pours & pours
South to North North to South we stand in different forms new forms new
forms

Migra con pistola, una riata y caballo
Border Guard Man with a Gun, a Riata & a Horse

con pistola en tu cadera y traje verde
with a gun by your waist and a green suit

y un caballo al galope
and a galloping horse

en la desembocadura del Río Grande
at the outpouring of the Río Grande

en el cruce hacia Texas — 16,000 corremos
on the crossing toward Texas — we run, 16,000

hombre de la frontera que estás lissenin'
border guard man, are you lissening

lavamos por las rocas
we wash on stones

entre las espinas
among thorns

agua suciedad de pie esperando
water filth on foot waiting

un trapo
a rag

nos secamos nuestros cuerpos limpios
we dry our body clean

anda tu
go ahead

el caballo
your horse

el arma es la ley
your gun is the law

es lo que dice la ley
thass what the law says

el mundo se derrumba
the world crumbles

migra de la frontera caballo
border guard man horse

escombros en el borde
borderline trash

sandalias masticadas dobladas rasgadas
bitten sandals chewed folded ripped

dónde correr
where to run

no me azotes como a una vaca
do not whip me like a cow

un cerdo azotando
like a pig thrashing

sin papeles
no papers

solo escape solo exilio
all is escape and exile

no me recuerdas
you do not remember me

techo de plástico bolsa de plástico
plastic roof plastic bag

entre la nada
floating through nothingness

un caballo y un látigo
a horse and a whip

todo lo que veo
all I see

mis hermanas lavan
my sisters wash

sus niños pequeños
their tiny children

al borde de ramas y piedras filosas
at the edge of branches and sharp stones

esperan paraíso
they wait for paradise

corriendo sin correr
running without running

vivir sin ser
living without being

jinete de la frontera con pistola acaso
border guard man with a horse maybe

se te olvidó que somos hermanos
you forgot we are brothers

se te olvidó que ella también es tu hermana
you forgot that she too is your sister

Poema de la frontera en cartón

tinta negra y pincel Japonés / cardboard
border poem, India ink & Japanese brush

J Feline
9/20/21
todos somos MIGRANTES
TEXAS you cannot forget me I cannot forget you we are one remember me
is this America is this America
15,000
16,000
17,000
BORDER
DEL RIO
INTERNATIONAL BRIDGE
SUFFERING ON THE TRAIL NORTH FROM MEXICO HAITI CENTRAL AMERICA FROM HUMANITY FROM HUMANITY HAVE YOU CUT YOURSELF FROM HUMANITY HAVE YOU CUT YOURSELF IN HAVE HALF WE ARE STILL HERE WE ARE STILL MIGRATING WE ARE STILL SUFFERING STAND UP FACE ME FACE ME FACE ME FACE ME NOW IN YOUR SHADOWS

Active Shooter

In memory of the beautiful children of Uvalde,
massacred in their classroom.

How did this happen
How did this happen

You are on the creeping fence
I am on the floor
Everyone is in the closet
The table what is it for

My friends are running
My friends are falling
My friends are calling
No one knows from where

No one is here
No one is there

How did this happen
No one is laughing down the stairs
No one is here no one is there

Police walk the halls
Police linger by the walls

the doorknob is still
it does not turn
it is open

Just the shooter shooting
Just the gun screaming
Just the bullet piercing

How did this happen
How did this happen
Everything is over
Everything begins

You are at the door
I am on the floor

Upside down
Upside down

How did this happen
Where is the world
Is this the world

I am on the phone with no one
All I have is love

Las Atenco Eleven

On board to Chicago. Front page and pages A-12, 13 of the NY *Times*.
Friday, Sept. 23, 2016.

One of the eleven on the front page raped beat captured contained in a
bus somewhere outside of your home town San Salvador de Atenco Mé-
xico stripped I will not repeat the story here the paper says your picture
says it your last strength your first strength again the last ten years of
blame the incarceration the lies your name hammered your family what
is left of it your university classes gone now that spirit you had a decade
ago you say gone the night feeling the dream-shamble the ghosts the
people who abandoned you your prison record for protesting the knives
inside the endless sighs the looking down the falling to one side of the
world the shut-down the secrets the realities kept to yourself the boiling
then the smoldering the violations the multiple violations the violences
the multiple violences the what is left of me's the formal badge strutting
the attack mouth speaker crony squad the reports doctored destructions
the fractures this standing body woman in gray scale you the criminal
with a criminal record paper weights the child daughter's drawings of the
police bloody and that thing called what do you call it you call it time the
ruins that other thing with an elegant name a social movement the pro-
test gone again that past that double past that keeps coming in gnawing
the present the fear heat sweat everywhere on the dripping doors the
floors the half-clouds the half-sky clouds peer down with the jaws agape
yet you stand yet you speak yet with a voice yet you here you are in dan-
ger again with the name of Barbara with the name Georgina and Claudia
with the name with the name Cristina with the name Yolanda and Norma
with the name Mariana with the name Ana María and the name with two

names Maria Patricia who looks like my mother who was beaten decades ago and one more with the name Patricia again on the front page you — you facing us still standing with all this standing still facing us facing each woman child woman child boy and man and police yes the Mexican president yes and the accusers and jailers and cronies and families severed and reunited some reunited in pieces and all the light all the possible light in the world you still standing you yes you stood up you rallied in La Plaza you were not afraid here now.

Nohemi—A Song for Paris

Mimi — can I call you that

this is a song for you —

with candles we stand & we kneel

this is how it is now we

send you these flowers across time

this time here which we

                    cannot explain

all love goes to you

& your friends the other night

so many with you gone we

stand we play Lennon's piano

Imagine — we say

a world without violence —

we want to imagine that in your name

Nohemi Gonzalez from El Monte

from Whittier, California from

Cal State Long Beach

then

        we run out of words

the words

so many words your mamá

Beatríz your cousin Jacqueline

we know them now — for you

we write them a poem too

I do not know how we will do that

we are doing that — that is all

like the designs you made — for a high-spirited world

you said you were *high-spirited & self-driven* — yes

like the dreams you had

& the words *First Generation*

the ones you used to

describe   your life

we continue with you — somehow

it is not important to know how

it is important to continue that is all

I must — say it again

we are all writing a poem

for you for your cousin Jacqueline

for your mamá Beatríz — she loved you

their love will make it alright

all of our love will make it alright   yes

                    here is my simple song for you Mimi —

We light Nohemi a candle

the candle waves across the stars

close they are so close

Nohemi & Paris are in our hearts

Because

          Nohemi &

                    Paris — are in

      our hearts

For George Floyd Was a Great Man

For George Floyd, RIP, and family, for all

For he was a wandering lamb trapped & lured toward the flames

For the flames were upon him for they would seal his story

For he was taken down face down body down to account

For his soul stood up & harkened the chariot song descending

For he pleaded as the fiery metals coiled upon his ebony skin

For he was our Renaissance our thirst our vessel for Freedom

For it is said he was our father our son our symbol our body

For a choir assembled on the streets in every furnace of witness

For he called upon his mother as he called upon the Source

For he was the ancestral ship burning through maps & chains

For he was the future no one had prophesied the Now & the Is

For he was taken in the evening as we noticed the power remain

Porque George Floyd era un gran hombre

Para George Flcyd, RIP, y su familia, para todos

Porque él era un cordero errante atrapado y arrastrado hacia las llamas

Porque las llamas estaban sobre él porque ellas sellarían su historia

Porque fue derribado boca abajo cuerpo abajo para rendir cuentas

Porque su alma irguió su alabanza hacia la carreta celeste descendiendo

Porque rogó mientras incandentes metales se enroscaban en su piel de ébano

Porque era nuestro Renacimiento nuestra sed nuestro canal hacia la Libertad

Porque se dice que era nuestro padre e hijo nuestro símbolo nuestro cuerpo

Porque un coro se reunía en cada calle en cada horno de testigos

Porque llamó a su madre así como invocó a la Fuente y a la Raíz

Porque era el barco ancestral ardiendo entre mapas y cadenas

Porque era el futuro que nadie había profetizado el Ahora & el Es

Porque se lo llevaron al atardecer mientras notábamos su luz permanecer

i Will Luv U 4Ever, Orlando

For all our 49 LGBTQ brothers & sisters massacred at the Pulse Dance Club, Orlando, Florida. RIP & their families & all the 53 injured & their families, for all seeking the end of homophobia & mad gun machines.

                    Let us go let us go   it is time now

from here to there & become   all
from polished hate to raw love &   love all
from lips to lips from love   to love

— in full freedom libertad tuyamía yoursmine   in bongó & bolero
Orlando present presente para siempre 4Ever Orlando in conga & timbales

lift her body in all color in red in yellow in white in black in brown in red
cuerpo de ella en color total en rojo en amarillo en blanco en negro en café en rojo
                                        how i love U
lift his body holy in brown in red in white in yellow in black
levanta su cuerpo bendito en café en rojo en blanco en amarillo en negro
                  como te quiero quiero con maraca y chékere

in blur in blur to blur
entre uno en medio entre otra nace uno sale otra
como te quiero quiero in rhythm eternal ritmo

            No hate no shoot no flames no screams on screams
         No shoot no night inferno night of crimson-blue & apart
            4EverNight

It could have lasted a whole song

It could have lasted w/ U & me going round & round —

Who is going to brush my arms up against the sky hermanito

who is going to shake my hips against the wavy light hermanita

who is going to leap rounder than these tumbler bullets striking tú y yo

who is going with the woman flying out the narrow crystals you & me

                    toward the flooded yellow-green exit

who is going to kiss kiss her shrapnel wounds sharpening

& catch her body twist & face down

at the Pulse — luv

loving life is that a crime (i ask you from here)

loving live is that a crime this time next time

        we shall not forget U Orlando

        (we shall march for U — Orlando)

     i will lovU 4Ever

Crossing Poland to Hope

There are bombs

T-72 battle tankers rolling in the purple dust

there are attack helicopters & missiles across the black sky

into the living building streaks burning

separate through the penumbra

torn wings torn shrouds from the void   it

unites us all into one thing one howl

where do you go now where do the people go now

from Ukraine the metro fills up children & elders

crying & stoic hearts you huddle you create a new society

for a moment underground

you are the Underground now

you have always been

underground nowhere a bag of bread

a tiny toy bear white & black   a woman says

"i woke up

to a world this morning

i never imagined"

you go you go there are few choices

a child presses your leg

you erase yourself chalk lines cut the sky again blue & black

almost holy almost angelic you hear a song & a drum

it is the song of emptiness it is the drum of timelessness

the people almost frozen wrapped in rags & woolens

to Poland

to neighboring countries

in buses some trains automobile lines again

crushed again a child hugs your legs in Moscow

woman protesting in the night pulled dragged

into a Filtration bus the last sounds

it is bravery it is hope it is the left side of the chest that

protests & drags into the steel

"Disarm & surrender!" the Russian ship speaker says

to the last ones on Snake Island guarding the border

they spit back & laugh

blasts and guns who knows what happened to them

do you

hope brave hope Ukraine thirst hunger Ukraine

men & women some behind windows some

en route to Poland some with Molotov fuel

inside a wine bottle there it goes thrown from

the seventh floor the youth almost falls with it

everyone face to face everyone in-between

the crumbling walls the crumbing flaming

T-72 battle tanks row after row then they turn back

there is no map no plan it is Russia lost & against itself

turning into the wall the tanks move backwards

surrounded they dissolve

a resistance fighter stands in front of the T-72

nothing no one knows inside the tank

where do you go when you are supposed to kill

what do you do when reality stands

in front of your T-72

it is the vortex of nothingness inside of you

it is your brother calling it is your sister wondering

who you are now

fire crosses the streets

burning light paints Santa Sophia church

below underground the peoples huddle in the basement

a child hugs your legs you are in a train

you are in a metro you are waiting for a T-72

there is a van a jeep a truck something

reshaped into metal thick accordions

its mouth opens no one just the people

underground & in a train & at the crossing

in a bus you get a bag of vittles something to eat

police surround you again in Moscow protesting

people applaud across the world

another T-72 is repelled toward an airfield in Kharkiv

look ahead right there

another military truck smolders next to a tree w/o leaves

another protestor in St. Petersburg he must be 20 or so

pulled apart by two police a body lies in a ditch

in Ukraine no one knows who it is there is no time

no direction just a breathing you wish you could

sit down with a bowl of steaming soup & a bread roll

at the edge of Kyiv Putin says he's considering

nuclear options you are in Ukraine everyone is

in Ukraine even though they are crossing into

Poland somewhere between everything

in motion high alert since this morning Kharkiv

& you & all frozen trees & soldiers behind steel sheets

a delegation meets Monday with Russians

at Belarus border how can we speak of borders

in the midst of T-72's fire in the skies

missiles AK-47s & Russian ships the world

applauds again the blueness above shatters

refugees & suitcases along the trail

a nuclear option comes up again day after day

we suffer we witness suffering we devise an end

we report the progress & the stillness of things

the earth squeezes onto itself smoke tangles

around your face you are brave there's a sickness

of occupation & colonization & takeover &

mass murder you woke up this morning you looked

outside you said you never imagined you

would rise to a world like this — you

cross into Poland to hope

back in the Ukraine soon a husband or your mother

Ukraine her name

Dawn Will Usher Me

<pre>
                                      bluish nets

to the edge of Ulysses   kneel kneel

i will kneel there i   will embrace glass shards

broken helms i will drift in tawny sails

of Van Gogh stars you   will notice me in my

meditations this is where we shall meet   down

down touching gold statues of unknown gods

there will be no rebirth

                                     our continuity will mark

five million ocean-lives   our genesis in spiral

volcanic shafts & space particles   feverish quests

plankton rushing splintered light from another

world's desires   we go down

                                          half buried deities

staring forever lacquer-brushed & scraped from

yesterday & yesterday within yesterday wounded

    or   is it timelessness
</pre>

La aurora me guiará

sus redes azuladas

hasta el borde de Ulises   arrodíllate arrodíllate

allí me arrodillaré   abrazaré las astillas de vidrio

timones rotos flotaré a la deriva en velas pardas

estrellas de Van Gogh tú   me conocerás

en mis meditaciones aquí nos encontraremos   abajo

abajo tocando estatuas doradas de dioses desconocidos

no habrá ningún renacimiento

nuestra continuidad señalará

cinco millones de vidas-oceánicas   nuestro génesis en espiral

pozos volcánicos y partículas espaciales   búsquedas afiebradas

plancton astillando luz

de anhelos de otro mundo   bajamos

dioses semi-enterrados

mirando para siempre lacado cepillado y raspado de

ayer y ayer dentro de ayer heridos

o   será atemporal

or is it simply your life   my life in ragged flow &

our race toward existence   it is nothing again within

nothing again it is

this vastness still a vastness this

multi-turquoise deep grasp

our will to become to

come into being are   we ready   did we find our way

through the jagged ascensions it was

always the song &   the singing the whirling

                                        & the leaping

the gasping & the bursting

                                        the fractal substances

of our birthing belly the infinite multiplications within

the infinite multiplication

                                this is our crimson oneness

                                the hidden duplications yes

the very last mirrors this Kali Yuga   bathing you

& me extracting the elixir &   the howl then you go

                            &   i bow

last reefs &

barnacled piers

bleeding galaxy & that is all there is   giving

o será simplemente tu vida   mi vida en flujo caprichoso

nuestra carrera hacia la existencia   no es nada de nuevo adentro

nada de nuevo es

esta vastedad aún vastedad este

azul verdoso profundo aferramiento

nuestra voluntad de llegar a ser

a ser en totalidad   listos   encontramos nuestro camino

a través de ascensos dentados estaba

siempre la canción y   siempre el canto el torbellino

                                                    y el salto

el soplido el estallido

                                                    de sustancias fractales

de nuestro vientre pariendo las infinitas multiplicaciones dentro

de la infinita multiplicación

                                          ésta es nuestra unidad carmesí

                                          las duplicaciones ocultas sí

lo último refleja a este Kali Yuga   bañándote

y yo extrayendo el elixir y   el aullido luego te vas

                              y   yo me inclino

últimos arrefices y

muelles con percebes

galaxia ensangrentada y eso es todo lo que hay   el dar

Libélula / Dragonfly

42

Translation to Spanish by Lalo Borja

Yo yo

no pude detener mis alas   i

could not pull back my wings

estaban enloquecidas dijeron vete vete vuela vuela

they were blown open mad saying go go fly fly

gritando a todo pulmón una música extraña

shouting out everything impossible a music so strange

incomprensible para muchos

secrets for many

en cuyas cabezas el ruido y la suciedad

in whose heads the shaking noise & the rotten mush

se mezclaban con el heno

mixed with the hay

y la gente escupía whiskey

& the people spat whiskey

derritiéndose con cerveza allá abajo

melting away with beers down below

ehhh ahhh ehhh ahh rubios brutales explosivos

reddish blonde brutal explosives ehhh ahhh ehhh ahh

cambiando de colores haciendo

flashing fast colors making

gran ruido y blandiendo cosas

all out screeching & brandishing things

untándome y tropezando en espirales desde abajo

smearing me & tripping over in spirals way down there

rodando y cubriéndose de niebla

rolling & covering up with mist

sobre aquellas montañas que no dejaban

over those mountains that just couldn't

de sacurdirse temblando y cayendo

stop dusting themselves trembling & falling

no pude parar ajá me dije

i couldn't stop ahah i told myself

mientras pasaba el arroyo chapoteando agua

while I passed by the arroyo splashing water

sobre El Mulato Chihuahua donde alguna vez

over El Mulato Chihuahua where once

papá Felipe chupó leche tendido bajo una

papá Felipe sucked milk laying down under a

pintona seria y flaca

serious skinny goat

y después salió volando desnudo hacia El Norte

later he burst out naked flying toward El Norte

con una bolsa de tortillas

with a bag of tortillas

un sombrero verde y un par de calzones

a green sombrero & a pair of underpants

pegajosos y agujereados de bala

gummy & bullet-scraped

las lámparas aleteando a medio derretir

lamps winging away almost dissolving

sobre calles derruidas hechas de fuego

over the gnawed crumbling streets on fire

Ya ya ya basta basta

Hey hey hey that's enough enough

mira el bebé perdido caminando entre los cactos y la niebla

see that kid walking lost among the cactus & the mist

con zapatos de goma cargados

with rubbery shoes crusty

de polen conduciendo a los pobres

with pollen leading the poor

a liberarse de sus cadenas

to free themselves from their chains

quise decirle ¡Sálvalos!

i wanted to scream Save Them!

pero tan solo pude eructar un vómito viscoso

all I could do was gargle & spit up a thick vomit

sobre las cabezas de los generales

over the heads of the generals

que cabalgaban en caballos de cristal

that pranced on crystal horses

con fustas de cuero y pistoleras de telaraña

with rawhide whips & spiderweb holsters

disparando sin cesar

shooting shooting shooting

para luego saludar militarmente al espantapájaros

just to cast a military salute facing the scarecrows

una calavera con ojo de azúcar dientes de azúcar

a skeleton with a sugar eye sugar teeth

y mejillas de azúcar cuyos ojos eran dos huecos sonrientes

& sugar cheeks & whose eyes were two smiling hollows

¡Sálvalos! le grité pero tan solo una neblina inmovible

Save Them! i squeaked but just an immovable haze

y minúsculas nubecillas de vómito cayeron del cielo

& tiny clouds of vomit slipped from the skies

sobre sus sables y sus barbas hirsutas

over their sabers & stringy beards

por un instante cerré mi ojo gigante

for a minute i shut my incredibly large eye

Soñe con Mamá María en el bosque de los gitanos

i dreamt of Mamá María in the forest of the gypsies

sirviendo sopa a los heridos con su guitarra

serving soup to the wounded with her guitar

soñé con otras libélulas que pudieron escapar

i dreamt with other dragonflies finding a way to escape

se hicieron verdes y así volaron libres

they changed to green & that way took flight & were free

fue entonces cuando aterricé cayendo

this was when i landed tumbling

sobre un camino pedregoso y me sentí más pequeño

over a rocky path & i felt so small

que los mismos gúijarros

small as the pebbles themselves

caí de nuevo y mis ojos quedaron enterrados

once again i fell & my eyes stayed buried

respirando a duras penas adherido a una rama

i could hardly breathe dangling from a branchlet

rebuznando y rebotando sobre un techo roto

honking & bouncing over a half-torn roof

en una batahola estruendosa

in a thunderous wave of battle

voy voy voy y escapo por entre los soldados

i go go go & escape through the soldiers

cuyos costales están repletos de hocicos de cerdo

whose gunny sacks are loaded with pig jaws

y cartas de amor que dicen

& love letters that say

goodbye adios amor y love y adios

& amor & adios & adios & amor

y rostros sangrientos de niñas campesinas

& bloody tiny peasant girl faces

cosiendo parches que flotan

sewing patches that float

en ríos al amanecer

in the dawning rivers

flores ensangrentadas regadas por la tierra

blood-sprayed flowers tossed across the dirt fields

entre los muertos

among the dead

desintegrándose al explotar desde hornos de dinamita

disintegrating as they exploded by the dynamite ovens

extinguiéndose en el gorjeo azul del firmamento

extinguishing themselves in the chirping blue of the heavens

The Enlightenment of William Shatner in Space

For Mr. Shatner

Earth & its tiny life permanent

particles   impermanent

it does not matter

at this height & the stars & the gone

vessel of oxygen that was ours

for a moment the dark void not

the infinite dark void that is

the cosmos

that is the rotations the galaxies

endless creative dissolution who

are we here

at the edge of light shell of life & death

you raise your hands

to your face the words fall

there are no words in the piercing glow

compassion only it

cannot be described that life

you cared for at times

the lives you cared for

at times

the abundant fragile temporary things

a crumb green of existence

for the moment

all you have is one   word

La iluminación de William Shatner en el espacio

Para el Señor Shatner

La Tierra y su diminuta vida permanente

partículas   pasajeras

no importa

a esta altura y las estrellas y el desaparecido

cántaro de oxigeno que era nuestro

por un momento el oscuro   vacío no

el infinito vacío oscuro   es decir

el cosmos

es decir   las rotaciones de las galaxias

disolución creativa infinita quienes

somos aquí

al límite de la luz cáscara de vida y muerte

levantas las manos

a tu cara caen las palabras

no hay palabras en el resplandor penetrante

solo compasión eso

no se puede describir   esa vida

que a veces te preocupaba

las vidas que te preocupaban

a veces

la abundacia frágil y temporal

migaja verde de la existencia

por el momento

todo lo que tienes es una   palabra

you cannot grasp it

it moves in front of you & alive somehow

in all of us who

will save all the lives below

who will save all the lives

in this sudden hurricane

where you see them   see us the shape of all

this

repeats itself for itself for itself

against itself new shapes emerge   you

said you noticed

oceans

of truth   the sudden eclipse

of the life

in darkness & light even if

in darkness   the only goal

no puedes alcanzarla

está frente a ti y viva de alguna manera

en todos nosotros quienes

salvaremos todas las vidas abajo

quienes salvaremos todas las vidas

en este repentino huracán

donde los ves   donde nos ves la forma de todo

esto

se repite por sí mismo por sí mismo

contra sí mismo surgen nuevas formas   tú

dijiste que te diste cuenta

océanos

de verdad   el repentino eclipse

de la vida

en la oscuridad y la luz aunque

en la oscuridad   la única meta

Mind Core

It considers those men that ambled &
Flushed their swords & cut off the neck
Of the blue horses & scraped off death
Dust from the carcass — rape of women
Tresses in boilers — the tin-colored animals
On the veridian grasses in particular the
Howler Monkey let the word shoot up
To the spheres — later we charged our
Blood with these accounts we hid the arms
Unforgiving texts & designs sewn into
Our tiny alabaster lockets. We visited
The last ridge where Victor Jara
Denounced the paramilitary — from
La Obrera in the heights of Tijuana we
Sketched the reddish moon & scratched
Poems those things that could carry
The letters we hauled on our backs.
We were separated from something we
Could not describe yet we were in
The Totality in the long winding turquoise
That broke us & put us back together
Again. What was that totality? It could
Not be written — *Green moon, green blood* —
We wrote. We marched to the ends of
Lacanjá Chan Sayáb & the heights
Of El Colorín — Central México. We were too
Late — the waters in which people bathed
Were cloudy & malignant — bellies
Bloated children leaned on the twig

House women stood up some sat cross-
Legged under the fire rays of noon —
We knew they knew the rubble land
Was not theirs or ours it was stuffed into
The cigarette packs of the Ladino
Hacendados who kicked up their short
Boots in the City of Bones below.
With our faces in new faces we rolled
Back to LA. Do you change it? Do you
Leave it the same?
Words — what are they?
A new cognition was required — then
With the the ecstasy of the unleashed
Other things pulled us apart. Other th ngs
Reassembled us
Now we are here.

Walking Notes (Tenochtitlán, DF)
with Francisco X. Alarcón, 1978

Coyolxauhqui

Excavations

downtown México DF here
archeologists bend down below us hard hats
women and men whispering swishing
brushes uncovering her stone armature body book revolution
sister. We walk on tiny quadrants of consciousness
protein stone disk criss-crossed by knowing and unknowing

we
move on
this is how two spirit wanderers walk to La Torre Metropolitana
swashbucklers in mega — DF

Elias Nandino in a tan suit "El Doctor" they call him "El Doctor poeta
de canciones de amor oscuro y popular" almost Pedro Infante in a fancy
scarf and wide pants he looks on
with chavos from Bellas Artes slamming together the next issue
of *Tierra Adentro*. Let's do an issue Francisco says
8 stories up above Tenochtitlán outside

we meet up with poeta Arturo Villafuerte

in his overalls I tell him
to read with some congas and a string bass get some soul
into it he nods ¡órale! who
knows what's next

so we go

who knows where we go and Arturo hands us his

new chapbook — *As de corazones* rotos says he has a column

in *El Excelsior* so we should send him some pieces no problem

la hacemos in the middle of this onda we run into Ernesto Trejo

huffing it down San Juan de Letrán with his mini-series of poetry

chapbooks — we hang for a while in the middle of the last qtr

of the century where I saw Macario a few blocks from here in the

early 60s searching for a hut to be able to bite into

an existential turkey leg this is the life on the street poeta a poeta

we walk on

tacos y cervezas blood chorizos caldos fried fish heads we head

to Gustavo Saenz's cantón in his mini Omni car bubbled up

to La Colonia Roma a light plate of burritas—

what on earth is a "burrita"

I ask

   Jamón con queso on a white flour tortilla like a

quesadilla Gustavo says in his neat bluish coat—

Francisco makes a deal

let's publish a Chicana and Chicano edition of *El Suplemento Literario*

that we'll edit for *El Excelsior* — What do you think Juan Felipe

la hacemos, I say.

   We walk on we move we rap we eat late near

Las Catacumbas bar we check out a teatro popular—

"La Traigo Dormida" a cardboard comedy

about how a husband hypnotizes his wife

we leave hustle to another day with Editorial Katun here's a

book on the life of Agustín Lara I think I'll get it for Alejandro

back in SF, Murguía has a thing about Lara
serrucho hacksaw face Lara his dark
melancholy jagged wooly skin his metaphysical attempt to stitch
everything that has been cut open back together again — that
cannot be stitched back together again like we are Azteca
Humpty Dumptys in the Promised Land Francisco I say

Wait a minute — stop

Why don't you write about your life ok?
Why don't you write about your love your alone world when
you come to Mexico by yourself that intensity the night
after night on fire why don't you write about your
real stuff (Why don't I)
Francisco keeps walking
I keep walking we walk like always dreaming out loud

Leaping bloody
Torn elegant magical proteins unambiguous new planetary beings
broken reassembled faces with a penchant to turn North then South
then North then South to be born reborn into what is does not
matter we know how to walk together the bus station
comes to view I have
to head back to Stanford somehow
No money no food just enough for a ticket to Tijuana
wave to Francisco I'll see you later
We'll start over the same way

Francisco dissolves into multiple audiences
I wave   we go

Ramón "Chunky" Moroyoqui Sánchez Played

In memory of Ramón "Chunky" Moroyoqui Sanchez, 10-28-16,
Logan Heights, Chicano Parque, SD, CA.

Chunky played his marimba
where there was shattered cement and broken glass
It was not easy Chunky moved forward day by day

Year after year Chunky played his cuatro
He played cultura the kind we knew the kind we dreamed
He plucked the notes we had forgotten the ones
that connected the lands we left long ago
with barrios we stood on the ones cut in half and into pieces

Chunky strummed the harmony the rhythm the starry life
we carried yet we did not sing out or know how
Chunky called out the samba but it wasn't just a samba

It was all of us together taking our land back
in front of bulldozers and carrying young trees
to their new origin to the front yard of our community house

Chunky stood tall with all of our colors and voices
Chunky sang deep for all of our suffering and peace
Chunky lifted us up with his spirit of kindness pouring

It was not easy it took many years until we all unfolded

Chunky never turned back he was a California Brown
Chunky kept on singing and teaching and speaking
Chunky gave us love and fire so we could continue

Gracias Chunky
We shall strum your songs of freedom
We shall continue en el camino

Tutu Sol – At the Underground Café

Lissen:

Ok, ok — okaaaay — so

I'll tell you all about me, ok? Then you can do whatever you want to do, I mean do not stick around just cuz you think we are friends all of a sudden. I am out to save the world. And I am gonna start with one person — my father.

Ok? Anyway — as you can see by gazing at me. Stop right there. I am into the word "gazing." Not "looking." "Looking" for is dummies, ok? "Looking" is like sayin' "kindergarten" or "kinnygarten" which is what people usually say. So why on Earth do people think they gotta say "Kinder"? Is that totally dumb? Where was I? Uh. Where was I? Uh, oh yeah. Ok. Okey. Uh. Oh yeah. Uh, look if you want to know me can you please just open your glorious watery eyes and tell me what you see? It's not hard to know me. What am I wearing? Ok? Got it? Ok. Yeah — check me out. Cropped top, the color of what? And don't say "yellooow." Everybody on this planet says "yellooow." And what else are you gazing at? It is not "red" on my hair either. It is pomegranate with cerulean blue. That's better. And my feelings? Oh yeah. "Feelings" huh? Well. I do not believe in those little wiggly things you label as "feeelings." I am all about colors. What colors are my pants? Come on! Don't just stand there. There's people behind you waiting to order their Macchiatos too. Thalo green-bean! Speak up. Jeez. What are you? Are you a fishing pier? Like the Muni Pier at the end of Van Ness and Bay Street? Are you getting a sense of my "Inner self" now? Yeah. Sure. Just gaze and you got me. Ok? And my hands. These are not tattoos. That is totally too committed for me. Ok. Got that? It's Henna. You you know that but you just do not notice anything. That is a mega-ballistic problema. By the way I speak Spanglish. How about my face or are you scared to gaze at my 15-year-old face! 15! Is that old is that young? Wrong! It is gruesome, crazy and tough as bat-crap. What about my face? Glasses, correct. Don't wanna hear about my acne, my face, my skin. Super dark brown. Hold it right there. "Dark" is totally out. "Dark" is political. Say *solar brown*. Cuz I am part sun-star. Stop right there. Look. My father, Silva, is from the central mountains of México. Indian. Stop! And that's the wrong word too — he is First People who believes when we die we become Sun Crystals. That's it. I do not believe in explaining myself. Ok? Got it. Jeez. My strength is what you see — 4' 9" of Sun Brown Power! Most of all — I am original. Not a cardboard girl. Not a weeper. Not a funny-bunny girlfriend. And — I don't whimper when I talk. You get it. I am sure. Sure. You just make your little life and I'll make mine. Uh-Oh. The line is getting shorter. There are so many people here at the Underground Café you can drown in people's sweat, hipster sweat. Just to let you know, ok? You are not going to see me dressing like a Hipster or whatever they call themselves. Los Ricos. That's what I say. Fashion and tight $300 pants are not my thing or the 300 flavors of shampoo like the girls love and fight about at District 24 High. My friends, well. Well. My friends are — I just got one friend. That's all you need. Her name is Aliss. Lives in a group home. Plays guitar like me too. We write songs and whisper them to each other. Leo Villa, that's another thing. She's a girl in case you got your genders all upside down like most people do — well, she is my arch-archest-enemy — might as well spit it out. She says she knows where she is headed. Oh, yeah. And she says she has a *plan* for her life. Sure. And she says she's better than me, smarter than me and that I better not get close to Parker Sanchez, the dude of her world. Or she will crack my skull on the curb of the Dolores Bus stop and scrub my face on the fence. Sure. She's a total weak creature with two frog-legs. If she just lifts one hand above her waist headed my way in the halls, she is mine! Are you getting the picture? Where was I? Uh? Ok? Us. Jeez. Uh. Ahh. Oh yeah. My favorite thing. Check out my satchel — what a dumb word. "Satchel." Said it so you can relate. Ohhhh yeah. Hehehe. You know what's in it. No. Not an apple, duffus! My writing journals and my sketchbooks! What else is there in the whole universe? Buying trinkets on the internet? Oh yeah...sure. Not me. I write. I draw. I am involved in the evolution of the planet because I am part solar star. Got it? Jeez. I am exhausted.

Don't think I am just bumming around ok — trying to get your attention!
Got serious things on my mind. Just last week things were totally different.
Was at the movies. The Galactic on Van Ness off of Market. Grabbing Lemon
Meringue from a white box while watching Despicable 3 with my papa. Does
not get better. Will never forget. It's gonna be my bestest memory. Monday
ICE nabbed him when he went to register. No papers. Mama, no papers. Me?
Papers. Don't pretend you know what that means. You don't! Just like the
words "looking" — you see nothing. Absolutely nada! You just skip around
thinking this big ol' world is a wavy, pink-striped lollipop. Guess what? It
isn't. It's a nuclear detention death trap set to go off at any second. Now what
am I gonna do without my papa? Who is gonna tell me all about the Tutu —
the messenger hummingbird? Like my name. You know what I am going to
do? Listen as hard as you can ok? I am going to bust him out of that stupid,
bozo, detention center! How am I gonna do it? Dunno? Gonna have to drop
out, probably. My mother is going to miss me so much. She's gonna burn a
hundred candles and chant to her Catholic and Aztec stone statues. Poor lit-
tle mama Alvina. And I am going to miss her so much it's gonna hurt my toe.
Now it's gonna get really bad. And if I blow it — gonna be in a big gray cube
for girls locked up forever. What shall I do? If only I knew how to live, I mean
really, really, truly live. Without half of me always on the verge of fading. And
the other half on the verge of exploding. That's all I want — to really, really
live. Uh. Where was I? Hold on a second. Before I order my last Venti Passion
on Ice, let me repeat something in case you are day-dreaming like everyone
here. You want to know how I am feeling?

Gaze at me for a second.

Come on! 92 million miles away Tauyepá, our Sun Crystal Whirler, is send-
ing me at this very moment ten thousand personal buckets of bronze-solar
blood. And right now it is splashing over me and coming down my eyes.

California Brown

Zoot Suit from San Ysidro

to the Klamath — wearing your drapes long cut coat
spaghetti belt flappy pants to the ankle
do not forget your calcos glossy pointed Staceys

& your tando

fedora black or gray or cinnamon or blue — if you can spot it
& the chain — let's not call it a chain for the moment
hooked to your pants your tramos & of course
you gotta have the ranfla ready that sharpened Ford
rumble seat skeletal green or midnight border howl
flecked paint bloody streak that solar wheel you touch to turn
& your skirt fenders where are you going Brown

There's a borlo up ahead
the East Los party — in the penumbra in between everything
       let's not call it a party let's call it

the place where you
become whole again
(I am not talking about the party) —
after that migrant long haul from Juárez or Juaritos to
El Paso or El Chuko or EPT toward Tucson or
Tuksón — meet up with Los Chasers then — wait my
time-space in this text is incorrect — in Juaritos
you become that Brown called a Pachuka or Pachuko
that nation-devourer why is it that
somehow you become infinite everywhere

let's get back to LA

to that Navy brawl they called the Zoot Suit Riots in '43
let's get back to now — you

                                                        in Juárez again you
in Tijuana again you are in that muddy tent

all the way from Guatemala — for the moment
there's tear gas — there's the Thing Sky Piercer El Bordo
or we could say the border — and the brawl

                        there's no brawl
you could call it a cell
a detention camp a chain sewn around you it is also termed
Separation & the ranfla you could call it the border bus
in white & blackened windows — wait

we have not talked about your transcendence
we have not talked about the forces of power
ripped into your bones & flamed out of your face
we have not talked about how things have not changed
& your seat on that white bus blackened windows
we have not talked about how things have changed that
odd-shaped radio cracklin' wrapped around your shirt buckle

        So:
let's talk about you California Brown

Notice: Stop Anti-Semitism

It is that simple

do you want to live in a spiderweb suit

w/a broken mirror why would you want to carry

the lies the Auto-da-Fe burnings

the genocide & smoke & gases?

why eliminate your humanity

why march into the Abyss

screaming the tawdry texts of the Abyss

Infinite suffering

is denying your sisters and brothers

is denying yourself

Do not feed the high-collar Serpent

stepping into its undulating sands of fires

The world is breaking, rumbling, meltirg

Being & Totality walking away from us

My mother Lucha

when we lived on the desert roads & trailer parks

campesino worker camps

knew — in the face of hatred:

Offer bread, friendship, sunlight & songs

Landing on Earth Tomorrow

The first thing i will do is feed the sparrows

i will kneel in front of the last trees & last

lakes & ask for forgiveness for all those years

of abuse & assaults, thievery & lies

                                        i will continue

i will enter prisons, detention centers and face

the shackled — we will bow to each other

we will share brown rice and steaming eggplant soup

we will remain quite and notice the ten thousand

pictures of mistakes and crimes blurring across our forehead

we will walk out with our eyes brimming salt water

our hands offered to each human being

i will enter the money house and dissolve all accounts

and redistribute sacks of gold dust to the homeless

those mumbling asleep on the corners of the

brilliant metropolis of tilting knife-sharp towers

i will continue stumbling & shouting & pleading

to Czars & Pontiffs, Marshalls & Generals, i will

offer them three sparrows & a bowl of seeds &

point to the flaming mountains — "This is your task

the earth does not know violence unless you

create it" i will tell them — i will continue

i will leave & amble away like my ancestors toward

unknown trails & wild new regions & waters — yes

waters —

there I will wet my face through roaring waves

of the last oceans & taste the tears of the all its

slimy creatures, "Forgive us" i will whisper & i will touch

their infinite scales & blood-leaf eyes — above us diving

gulls will ask, "Who are you?" i will say "Nobody"

"Nobody cared for you — a few continue" — then

i will return to my planet still gnashing its levers &

assembling its odd shaped powers "Tomorrow somebody

will arrive" i will say to the creatures & the starving &

the sparrows — the very last sparrows."

HOLLER / GRITO

In memory of Tyre Nichols & Alonzo Bailey, Rest in Power & so many killed w/o a cause

Tyre

we become you we

pummeled kicked down asphalt kicked again
choked chased

tasered shot whipped sprayed again dragged

        policias w/ kevlar w/badge w/stripes
w/Glock w/ thick jackets glance
— once sisters once brothers

                [Daunte Wright]/RIP

once our brothers once our sisters
they come forth they step back
last dance on Castlegate Lane corner

        Memphis, Tennessee

                [Breonna Taylor] RIP

houses on the block quiet
lawn grasses turn to you
sharpened by the mower

                [Atatiana Jefferson] RIP

we hold you up
we are here with you
bluish folds of night darkens

                [Aura Rosser]RIP

                    Tyre
we become you
tonight falling & slide down
cop car door

broken we lift you up
miles away we hold you
we are here here

[Stephon Clark]RIP

you fall to the right
we lean to the right
you lean to the left you fall to the left
Tyre gone now

[Philando Castile]RIP

we wipe away your blood
swollen forehead
chest busted
heart kicked
Tyre Tyre Tyre you will not perish
you will not
fall again

[Alton Sterling]RIP

we carry you through green mist
we bring you home we wash your splintered
swollen body burst
inside we take you to Mama
thousand miles out & millions

cry w/our voices
w/our lives
set upon you   you

[Freddie Gray]RIP

love is infinite
gardens blossom Tyre
w/your last breath-sounds

your voice is our voice

[Janisha Fonville]RIP

we offer our gathering
our skateboards
rough painted torn sky brave
colors of street fire

[Michelle Cusseaux]RIP

[Tamir Rice]RIP

[Michael Brown]RIP

this caldron of massacres
shootings & stabbings & bullets
the firing hand the choking hand
    the kicking boot the taser ring fingers at hand
whipping stick whipping
carving your back as if in slave time
[this time] :: gun hands same hands
so many violent Americas

[Tanisha Anderson]RIP

we become you we carry you
we write you poems
hit the high G's in the night choir

[Andre Hill]RIP

we carry you home
wet streets flaming boulevards

we are calling all
trains of Freedom

[Manuel Ellis]RIP

here we stand now
brave & determined
Saturday morning breakfasts
like in '68 & '69
murals of unity — Peoples' Parks
sufferings of history

we remember John Brown
we remember Frederick Douglass
we remember & sing their names
your name so many names

[Botham Jean]RIP

we continue Tyre
today we carry you

this is our truth now
cornerground & underground

each night flower a song
each song a night candle
each night candle a poem
each poem a night circle
each circle a people
all people all America

we holler Coltrane

your vastness across this Earth
we will plant kindness we will plant compassion
take the seed of friendship & humanity
to every house a *Love Supreme*

a Giant Sequoia rises below the fenders & breaks
out of the asphalt its impossible arms &
takes account with its impossible eyes
there
will be

no traffic stops no batons
no kicking boots no frenzied tasers
no hungry Glocks no melancholy AR'S
no bear sprays to death no plantation sticks
we will light & heal all the broken bodies
we will be marching together

[Akai Gurley]RIP

For Those with a Gun, a Taser, a Night stick,
& Coiled Vestments of Power When One Moonbeam
on the Broken Corner Was Enuf —
Once we were brothers sisters
when did violence unfold its volcanic shafts
its tentacles its coils & take you?
Why did you slash the Circle of Oneness?
Now you leave us bleeding on the edges
of all things

[George Floyd]RIP

[Alonzo Bagley]RIP

70

Tyre
lead us to our new home
our non-violent America our true Freedom
with you we will become the infinite circle
the New America your name in every sunrise

      winds pass through trees
          leaves turn Tyre
              doves wait on limbs
                  earth shakes the earth

                      this is when we shall holler

                          TYRE NICHOLS ¡PRESENTE!

                              true America
                              America Verdadera

PRONOUN(CE) ME

Alone alone w/my guitar alone with my turquoise
notebook with superheroes climbing over
w/ crazy faces skinny &

                                        my inky drawing pens
there are a thousand things splattered on my notebook
nobody pays attention nobody or cares besides
it is my notebook but but but
you would think i am nuts you already think i am nuts you always think i
am wrong what are you you don't even like my pronouns **THEY THEM** my
personal words
i feel close to my pronouns **CLOSE** — How am i feelin' ?
CLOSE to my pronouns **THEM THEY**

                                        alone alone

my red guitar
my turquoise notebook
scribbly cartoons
superheroes crazy wacky spooky faces buildings roads people zig-zagin'
soft lead pencils like in high school

other things in my notebook but but you
would think i am crazy crazy
actually actually you do think i am crazy
you think i am wrong wrong wrong
all the time do you know how it feels
to be labeled a wrong human person

                                             So i take off
                                             at midnight
                                       no one sees
                          me
knows me
talks
to me
cares
for me
speaks to
me

you take away my books
you ban my books you ban my teachers from teaching my books
i go there to feel close to things
things close to me
do you know how that feels you you ever been
evicted from the planet?

where are you
do you know who you are

So
i go out at midnight
tía's car i know where she keeps the keys
i drive

when no one is awake no one sees me no one knows me but but
it is me burning through a forest of eyes shut
it is me & my pronouns my jacket my boots & my hair razored
short short

Midnight me
i am my own Second Amendment
i am the Freedom everyone drools about i melt

through street lights
penciled posters stapled flyers
& turns twists & brakes sirens dark shops with CLOSED signs
neon snakes & unfinished bridges my old school Rage High &

i think of my grandmother's endless plate of quesadillas &
toast in the morning jelly and butter she is gone now
she knew me she knew me i was not a dirty thing
i was i
my my pronouns were my pronouns

                                            i existed

i park the car not far from my house
a razored hill
see crystalline rings of this endless city
all of its blurring lives i race the car until it stretches
under the moon & screeches & spits dirt & stones to the edge
overlooking the Strip on Sunset of nervous blinkers
heading to the Whisky & down down there parlors of nowheres

i am Them i am They that is all i need to say tonight.

i am almost
home
now

neighborhood
of gray gray
folded houses of
papel picado
spliced
sharp triangles cut by scissors you you
ever heard midnight scream?   You don't want to hear it

it screams something like a car crash split
into a gazillion faces &
shredded pants & icy tears & yanked plants on the sidewalks

maybe

you'll hear my music one day maybe
you'll see me dancing facing my tall m rror
where I can be them where they all
all are alone
my reflections & songs cartoons, notes next to the brown sofa
where i sleep
i lean on books by Pessoa & Jeffers Alarcón
Rigo Gonzalez H. Melt & Robert Frost & Nat Diaz

Pessoa has five souls
from his house of stone Jeffers listens to the gulls scream
Alarcón is on fire yet he speaks of love
Gonzales writes for they & dresses them at a Quinceañera
H. Melt tells they story of the city   my story
Natalie Diaz wanders through the Mohave searching gemstones
Magnetite under the dawn's lodge
Frost calls on the thawing southwesters to
"give the buried flower a dream"

                              i am that flower
                              i am that dream
                              i am that fire
                              i am that scream

                    (Remember everything I've said)

                              Can you pronounce me —
                              i am They in the Now
                              i am Them tomorrow
                              i am the singer
                              i am Thou

Notes / Credits

"We Shall Build a New House Green"

The Global Conference sponsored by Health Care Without Harm and focusing on developing green hospitals w/o plastic and other toxic materials called on me to write a poem on the subject and later I was invited to record and film the same poem for the United Nations Climate Change Conference (COP27) held in Sharm el-Sheikh, Egypt. This was the poem. I am very thankful. Poems can touch the earth and future in crises.

"For George Floyd Was a Great Man"

The form of this poem was influenced by Christopher Smart's (1722-1771) poem, "Jubilate Agno" written in a form derived from the biblical psalms. Smart's rendition moved me; it possesses depth, precision was most elevating. I felt the person and brutal story of George Floyd deserved such light, technical challenge and tone. I wrote the poem with deep respect to George Floyd and his family.

"SunRiders"

Hal Levison, director of the NASA Lucy Mission into space (Un-crewed, robotic, interplanetary spacecraft mission to investigate the three Trojan asteroids near Jupiter and eventually to the sun, Rocket launch, Fall 2021) invited me to write a poem to be engraved on a plaque and to be installed in the spacecraft. The plaque contains poems by other laureates and pioneers in various fields. Once in orbit, after hundreds of thousands of years, the craft's plaque is to be collected by a future generation and read. The reading is a telling of our current state of affairs on Earth and as an inspiration / warning verse to guide the hearts of our future planetary family. I am very grateful to Hal and his team for the invitation and such an accomplishment. We are all "Sunriders," moving as the sun moves, being inspired by its gifts of light and healing others with the gifts of our hearts. Thank you, Hal!

"The Enlightenment of William Shatner in Space"

On CNN, as I noticed the physical and verbal response of William Shatner's return to Earth after the landing of Jeff Bezos's Blue Origin's New Shephard rocket ship on 10/21, it occurred to me that Shatner in experiencing the crevice between life/light and death/darkness, had been tossed by "enlightenment," something that cannot be described, yet, he expressed it without knowing it. A mega-great moment for him and all of us.

"Poema de la frontera en carton"

Tinta negra & pincel Japonés/ Black India Ink w/ Japanese brush on found cardboard. Cardboard is one of my favorite mediums for writing, sketching and sculpture.

This is a cartonera Cardboard art poem — related to the "Gun and Lasso" poem about a recent influx of Haitian and Mexican and Latin American migrants. When incidents of border crossing take place and migrants are met with violent force and personnel, I feel a great need to write in various modes, ink, cardboard and computer. Recently, I have moved on to visual cardboard art. In short, I must write and disseminate the work. I do not believe in incarcerating and "returning" those that are suffering, in pain, starving and facing incredible record-breaking heat waves. Humanity is first. Ideology is not a value.

"Mahler — Son on Borne of a Street Song"

J.R. Cassidy, director of the Kentucky Symphony Orchestra invited me to write a poem in conversation with the life of the great composer Gustav Mahler (1860-1911) and his last magnificent symphony #9 in D Major. It was an extremely challenging task. Yet, I met it head on. As I listened to the symphony I was swept into its oceanic forces, galactic panoramas and most of all, its howls of life, true life, life itself. I thank Mr. Cassidy and the musicians of the Kentucky Symphony Orchestra. With deep gratitude.

"Active Shooter"

With all respect to the families of the children and teachers massacred and wounded — and communities of Uvalde, Texas. With Amor. Ban "Long guns."

"Mural Poem on 'Mural' by Jackson Pollock"

Curator of Special Projects, Mr. Derek Nnuro, invited me to write a poem relating to the University of Iowa's Stanley Museum of Art forthcoming Pollock exhibit. In particular, we talked about Jackson Pollock's "Mural" painting. Being a graduate of UI's Writer's Workshop and fan of the old and new Art library and Art museum's exhibits while I attended the university, it was a most inspiring request. Thank you!

"Notice: Stop Anti-Semitism"

I thank Tom Lutz for helping with this poem. Punctuated like the pianist, writer, artist that he is.

Gracias to Mai Der Vang & Anthony Cody that gifted me with a blurb for this collection — much gratitude.

Many gracias to the designers of this book, Carlos Espinoza and Shady Peak. Gracias to Andrea Sifuentes, who helped edit the Spanish versions of these poems.